Taking a Stantis

A Cartoon Collection by Scott Stantis
Editorial Cartoonist of The Birmingham News

Published by The Birmingham News Co., Birmingham, Alabama

ISBN: 1-57571-008-0

Printed in the United States of America

Dedication

In memory of Marc Robert Stantis.
I hope I'm still making you proud.

And always, to Janien.

INTRODUCTION

WHEN I GIVE TALKS A QUESTION THAT FREQUENTLY COMES UP IS:

HOW DID YOU GET TO BE A CARTOONIST?

CONTRARY TO POPULAR BELIEF, HEAD TRAUMA IN CHILDHOOD IS NOT AN ISSUE... I THINK.

I CAN'T HELP IT. HE'S SLIPPERY..

4 MORE YEARS?

OUT!

I EVENTUALLY ENDED UP IN CALIFORNIA WORKING FOR A STATE ASSEMBLY-MAN AND THINKING OF GOING TO LAW SCHOOL AND A LIFE IN POLITICS

GROWING UP IN A HOUSE WITH THREE OLDER BROTHERS EXPOSED ME TO ABUSE OF POWER.

HEY! THOSE ARE MY TATER-TOTS!!

NOT ANY MORE!

POLITICS WAS A PASSION IN MY HOUSE WHEN I WAS GROWING UP. THIS LED ME TO WORK ON REPUBLICAN CAMPAIGNS, WHICH WASN'T THE MOST POPULAR THING TO DO IN MADISON, WISCONSIN, IN THE '70's.

California Campaign Management College

SADLY, THIS IS THE ONLY DEGREE I HAVE.

THEN ONE DAY I PICKED UP A COPY OF THE COLLEGE NEWSPAPER.

THIS CARTOON STINKS!

I'D ALWAYS LIKED TO DRAW AND THOUGHT I'D ENJOY GIVING EDITORIAL CARTOONING A SHOT.

I ASKED THE EDITOR IF I COULD GIVE IT A TRY AND HE SAID:

SURE. WHATEVER...

WHAT HAPPENED THE NEXT WEEK CAN ONLY BE CALLED AN EPIPHANY.

I KNEW THEN AND THERE WHAT I WANTED TO DO WITH MY LIFE. I DREW ALL THE TIME. (YOU CAN IMAGINE THE EFFECT THIS HAD ON MY LOVE LIFE...)

I SOUGHT OUT CRITIQUES BY THE GREAT CARTOONISTS.

I WOULD NEVER TELL SOMEONE NOT TO BE A CARTOONIST BUT HAVE YOU EVER CONSIDERED ANOTHER LINE OF WORK?*

* ACTUAL QUOTE FROM THREE TIME PULITZER PRIZE WINNER PAUL CONRAD OF THE L.A. TIMES

UNDAUNTED, I CONTINUED TO DO WHAT I LOVE. I'VE LOST A FEW JOBS. LEFT OTHERS. YET, AFTER ALMOST TWO DECADES I ADORE WHAT I DO AS MUCH AS EVER...

I'M GOING TO DRAW THIS GUY'S NOSE SO BIG!!! HEE-HEE-HEE-HEE-HEE-HEE.

The World

According to Stantis

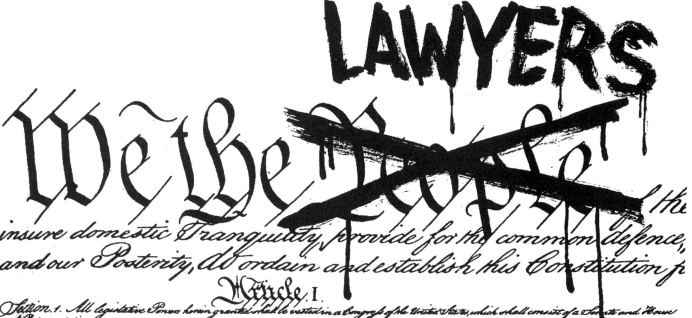

10

11

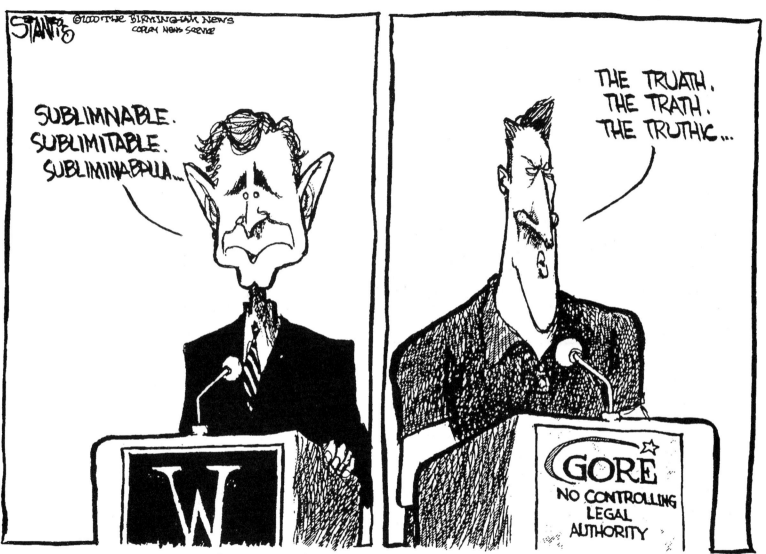

13

BALANCING THE TICKET

When all else fails, pick the clean guy.

AN EYE FOR AN EYE FOR AN EYE FOR AN EYE FOR AN EYE FOR AN EYE.....

STANTIS ©2000 THE BIRMINGHAM NEWS

SO LONG, COACH KNIGHT

16   Coach Bobby Knight, the insufferable basketball coach for Indiana University is, at long last, fired.

17

THE KISS

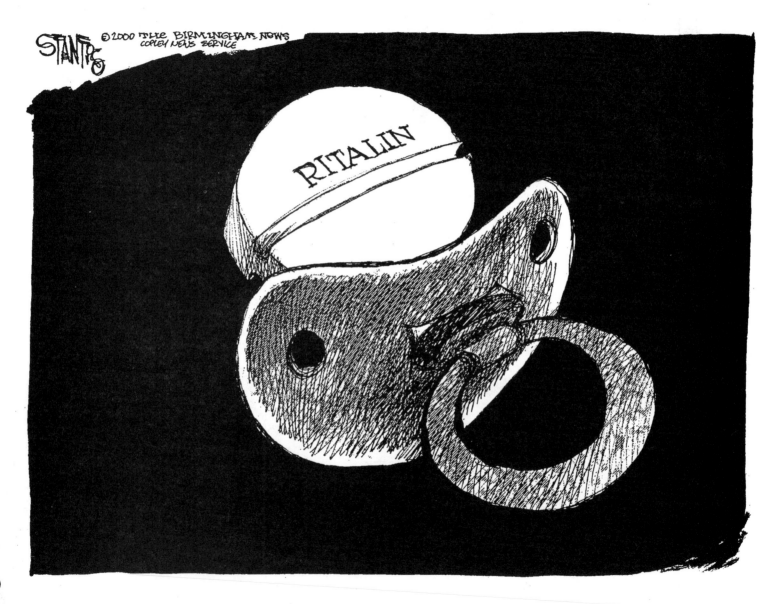

THAT'S ONE...

This cartoon ran one week before the Elian Gonzalez raid.

23

The story of Elian Gonzalez will drag out throughout the year.

25

27

STANTIS ©2000 THE BIRMINGHAM NEWS
COPLEY NEWS SERVICE

29

30   Jon Benet Ramsey's parents take a lie detector test under conditions that raise more questions than they answer.

Attorney General Janet Reno orders a dawn raid by armed storm troopers to break down the door of Elian Gonzalez' Miami home and whisk him away.

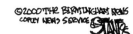

33

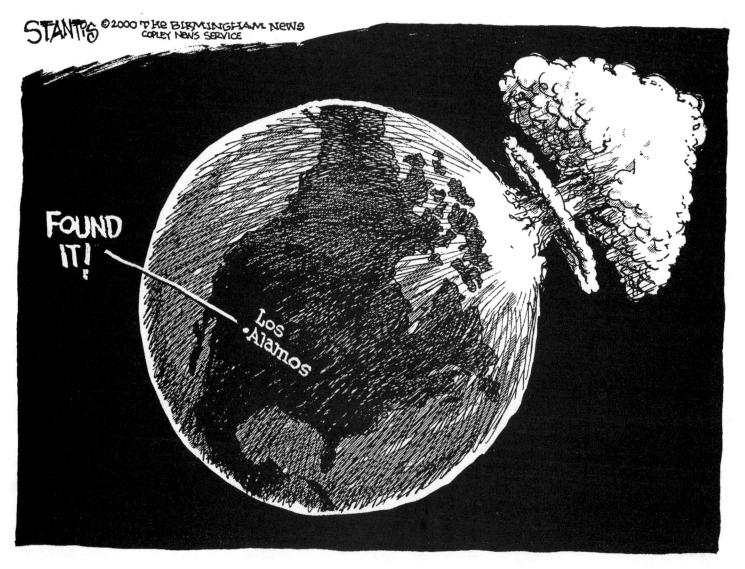

Nuclear weapons lab is "missing" a bunch of secret information.

A rash of hackers breaking into sensitive areas calls for serious action.

LET THE PUNISHMENT FIT THE CRIME

John Rocker, a pitcher for the Atlanta Braves, confirms just how stupid we all know jocks can be.

Taiwan threatens to declare itself an independent nation. Mainland communists disagree.

39

Elian is returned to Cuba.

THE TORCH HAS BEEN PASSED...

47

48

51

First Husband Bill Clinton pardons Puerto Ricans convicted of terrorism in the faint hope it will help his wife's Senate Campaign.

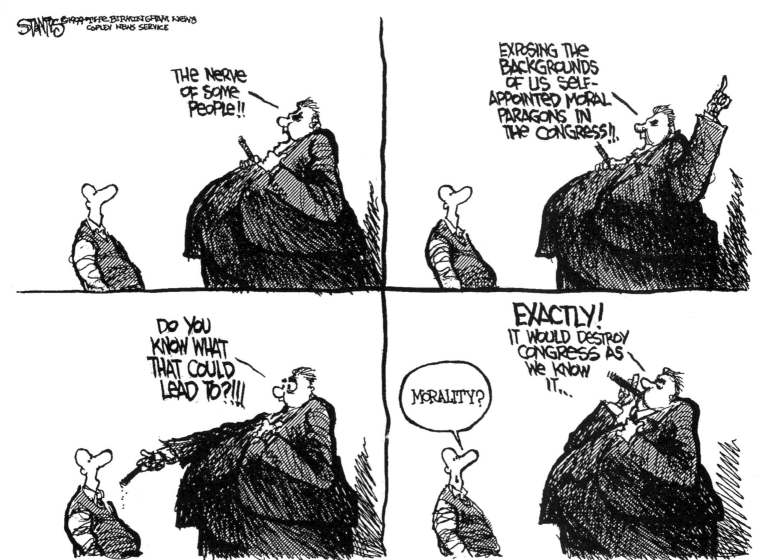

53

55

...as well as whom to blame.

PRIORITIES

59

62   Michael Jordan retires.

The Mars Lander disappears as reason does during WTO meetings in Seattle.

THIS IS PBS

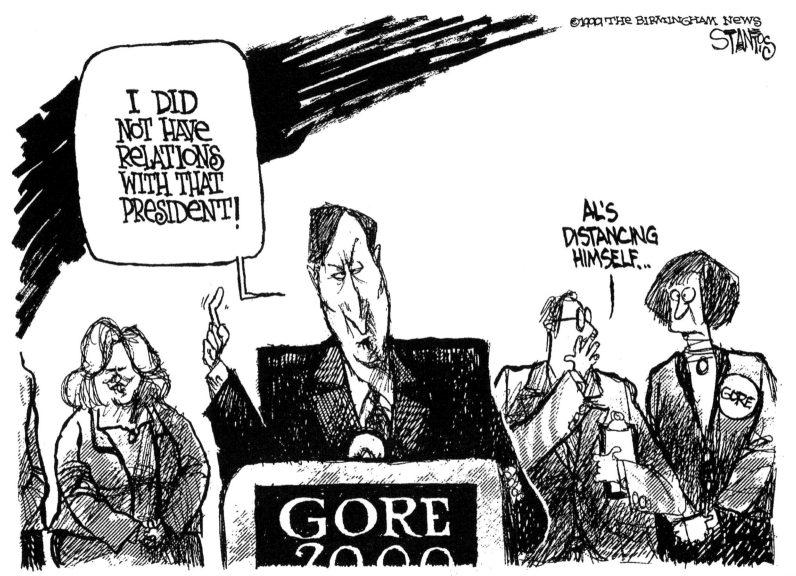

68

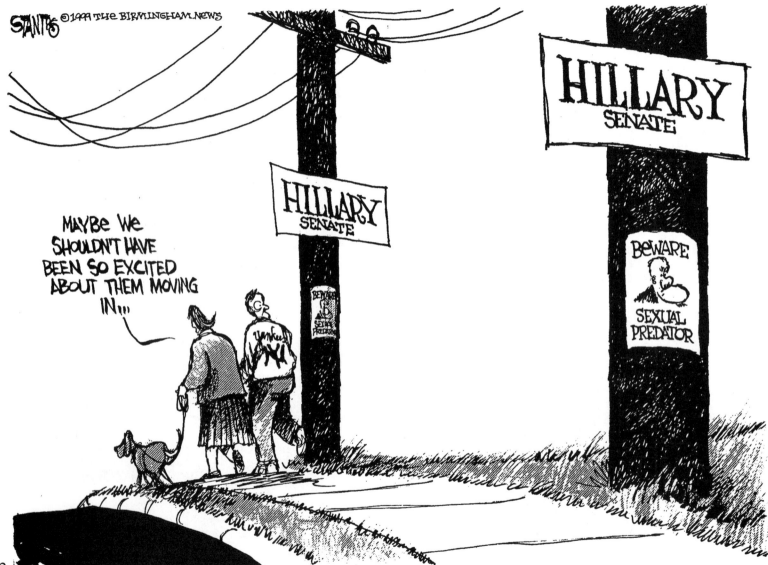

73

GOAL!

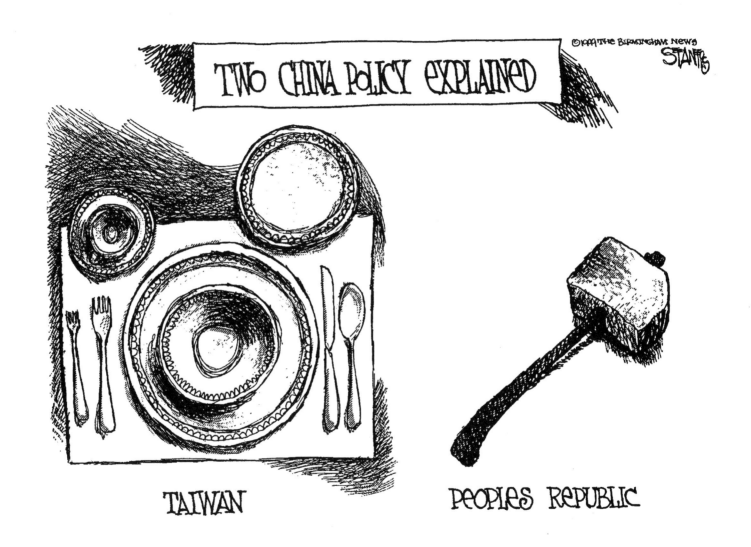

TWO CHINA POLICY EXPLAINED

©1999 The Birmingham News

STANTIS

TAIWAN

PEOPLES REPUBLIC

Justice Blackmun, author of the Supreme Court's Roe v. Wade decision, dies.

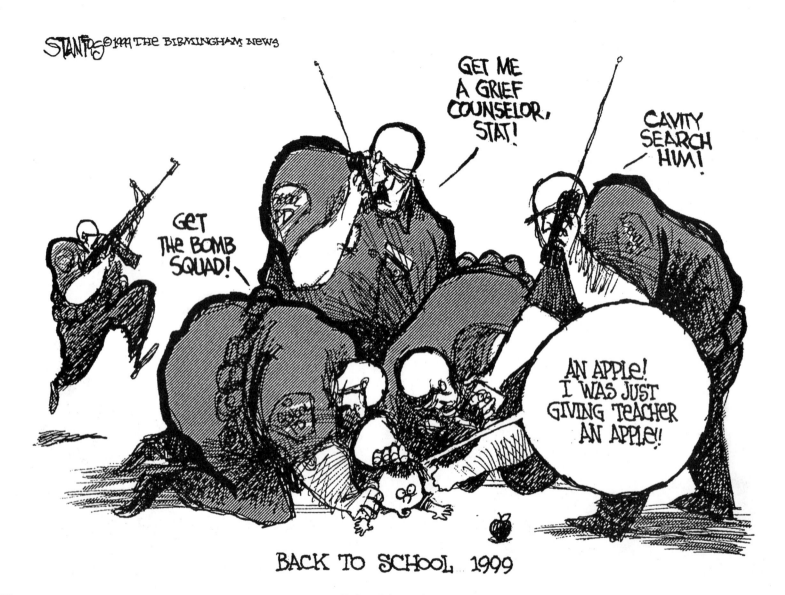

BACK TO SCHOOL, 1999

Columbine's legacy.

PARENTING 1999

The horrors of Columbine make us question our own family values...

TRYING TO PIECE IT TOGETHER....YET AGAIN

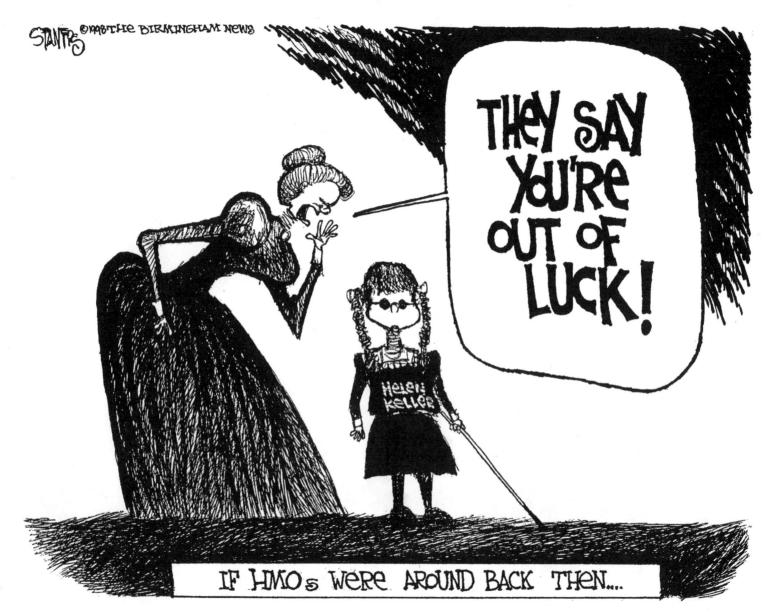

93

GREAT MOMENTS in U.S. FOREIGN POLICY

THE AMERICAN CONTINENTS...ARE HENCEFORTH NOT TO BE CONSIDERED AS SUBJECTS FOR FUTURE COLONIZATION BY ANY EUROPEAN POWERS.

MONROE

SPEAK SOFTLY and CARRY A BIG STICK!

TR

BEATS ME, CALL THE U.N....

STANTIS ©1998 THE BIRMINGHAM NEWS COPLEY NEWS SERVICE

SPLITTING HARES

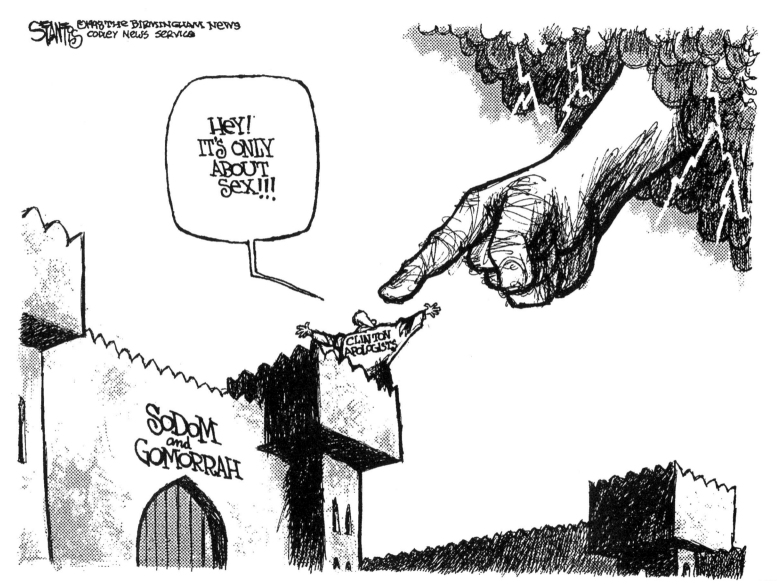

105

108

HAPPY 25TH ROE VS WADE

UNFORTUNATELY, THOSE DIRECTLY AFFECTED COULD NOT ATTEND...

111

STANTIS © 1993 THE BIRMINGHAM NEWS
COPLEY NEWS SERVICE

BYE
AMERICAN

U.S. JOBS

McGWIRE

ASTERISK

114

116

117

123

BUNGEE MARKET

125

THE GREAT RECONCILER – PERT' NEAR...

131

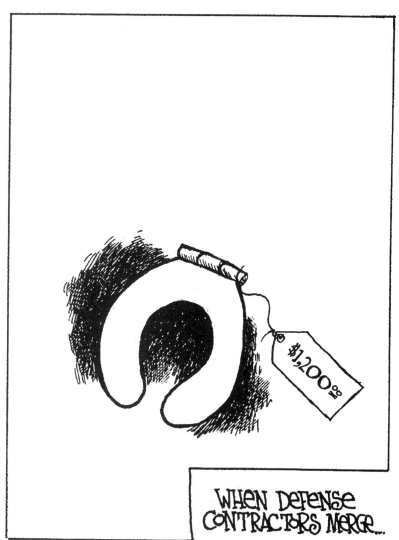

This is the first editorial cartoon I ever did for *The Birmingham News*

135

Alabama
According to Stantis

UNBEARABLE

DAY BEFORE LA. TECH GAME.

DAY AFTER LA. TECH GAME.

DAY AFTER FLORIDA GAME.

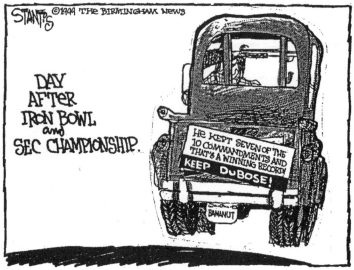

DAY AFTER IRON BOWL and SEC CHAMPIONSHIP.

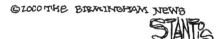

139

FROM THE FOLKS WHO TEACH OUR KIDS MATH...

Jefferson County Schools misplace $50 million.

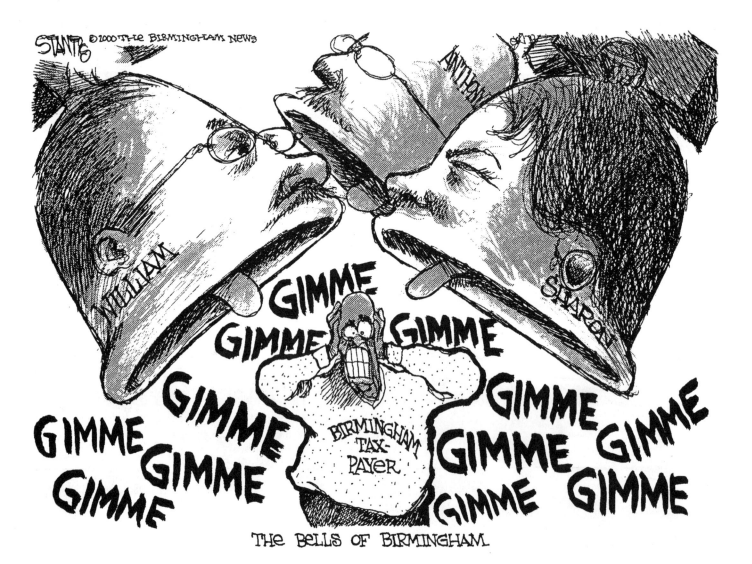

THE BELLS OF BIRMINGHAM

William Bell's family tries its hand at going on the government dole. First, wife Sharon sues the school board, then son Anthony by applying for a seat on that same board.

Governor Siegelman proposes a law requiring students to use courtesy titles. The problems in Alabama schools lie somewhere deeper than manners.

Governor Siegelman answered the call for reform in Alabama.

145

148   The state Parole Board, through ineptitude, release very dangerous persons with great frequency, it turns out.

LET'S HOPE HE GROWS INTO IT

Mayor Arrington resigns to let William Bell have a crack at the job before the election.

One of Fob's last acts as governor is to snatch much needed aid from tornado-ravaged Oak Grove and give the money to an aviation school in Mobile.

Then he commutes the death sentence of a woman who tortured and killed a young woman by injecting her with Draino.   153

Congressman Earl Hilliard travels to Libya, still unexplained, would give anyone pause.

The Birmingham mayors race run off drones on...

157

Bernard Kincaid is elected mayor of Birmingham

DON'S NUMBER COMES UP...

The lottery loses...

...and it's back to the drawing board.

163

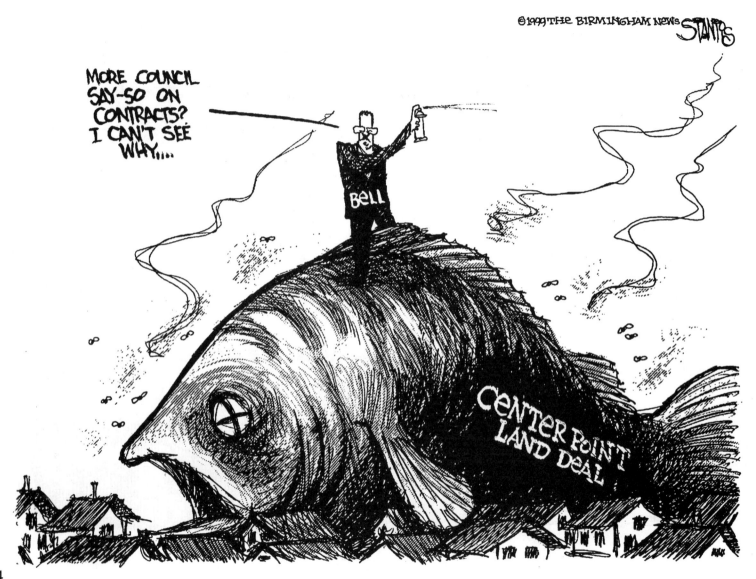

165

"URP.... NEXT!"

Terry Bowden is fired.

168   The early Republican choices in the last governor's race.

169

We're still waiting for Jimmy Blake's counter plan...

State Personnel Directory Halycon Ballard was found guilty of shop lifting.

©1998 THE BIRMINGHAM NEWS
STANTIS
THE BEAR BRYANT?!? WOW!! HERE'S YOUR BALLOT...
VOTE
WE NEED VOTER I.D....

THOSE LAZY, CRAZY, HAZY DAYS of SUMMER...

Birmingham's air quality is enough to make the famous iron man choke.

DON SIEGELMAN ANSWERS ALL OF THE TOUGH QUESTIONS FACING ALABAMA

The Republican run-off gets nastier and nastier.

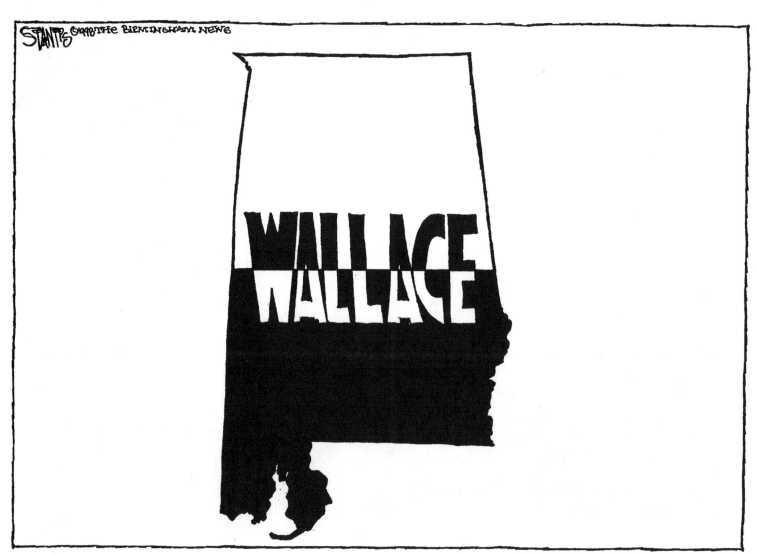

INDELIBLE

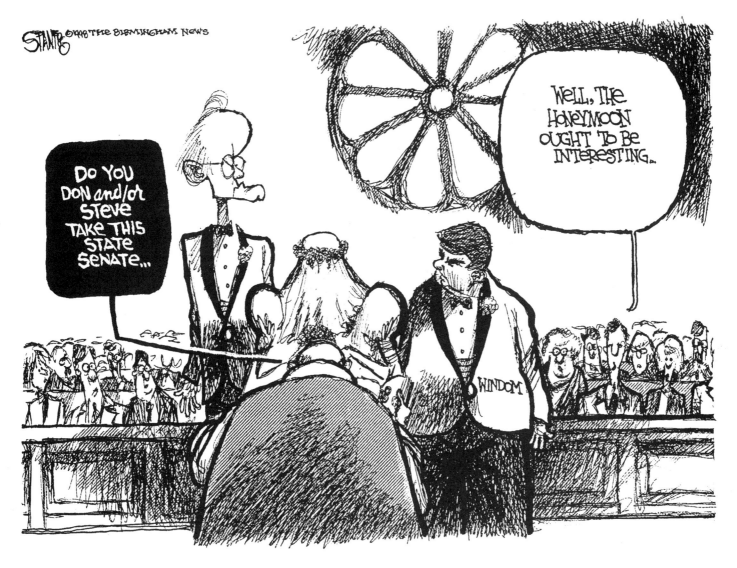

Democrat Governor Siegelman and Republican Lt. Governor Windom fight to control the Alabama State Senate.   179

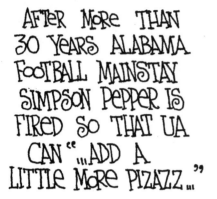

The Voice of Alabama Football is silenced.

Judge Ira Dement offers a reasoned approach to religious issues in public life. Reason has never been a word used to describe Fob James.

THE ROAD LESS TRAVELED...

184

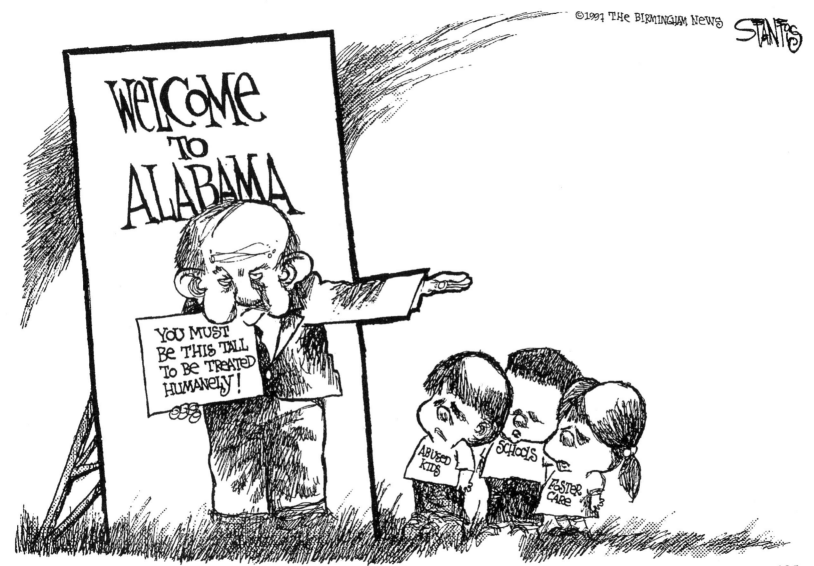

©1991 The Birmingham News   STANTOS

WELCOME TO ALABAMA

YOU MUST BE THIS TALL TO BE TREATED HUMANELY!

ABUSED KIDS

SCHOOLS

FOSTER CARE

185

186 Martha Nachman, Fob James' incompetent appointment as head of the Department of Human Resources, begins her bumbling and cruel tenure.

RUN FOR THE BORDER

THE SCHOOLHOUSE DOOR - 1997

188

Jewish kids in Pike County public schools are forced, physically, to bend down their heads in teacher-led Christian prayer and write essays on "Why Jesus is my friend," making for a wonderful argument against state-run religion.

The teachers' union fights background checks for teachers.

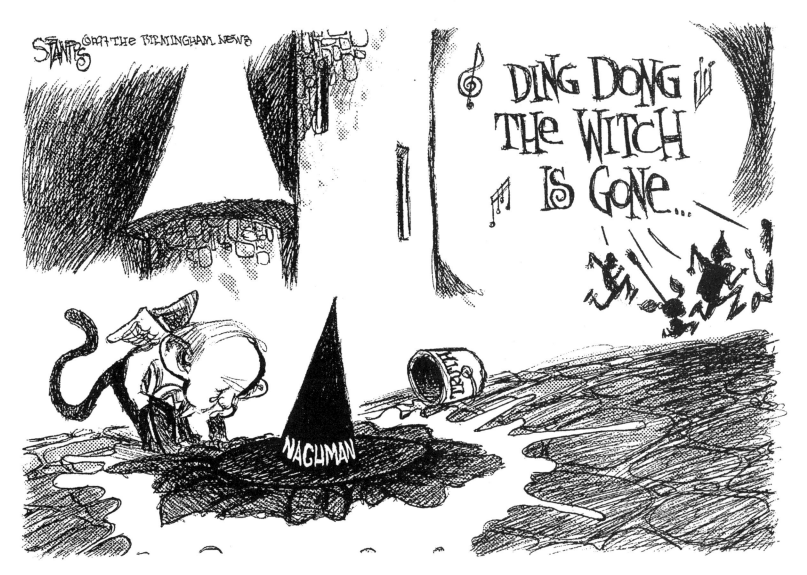

A bogus decree from UCLA sends Martha Nachman down.

Basketball star and Auburn alumnus Charles Barkley threatens to run for governor.

Newly appointed state Attorney General William Pryor, on leaving a court room where he argued against the R.C. decree, was quoted as saying, "My job is not to defend abused children." He has since learned differently.

"ANYONE?..."

The first appearance of "Tinker Fob."

A SHOTGUN WEDDING WE'D LIKE TO SEE...

Governor James says that shotgun weddings ought to be a part of welfare reform.

THIS IS WHERE THE PRAYER PART COMES IN...

In front of a group of Baptist ministers, Gov. James says "What kids need today is a good butt whooping and a prayer."   203

FINALLY, BAMA AND AUBURN FANS SEE EYE TO EYE...

Acknowledgments

In the course of a twenty-year career there are a slew of people who offered a guiding hand through a dark night to help me along. To avoid offending any of them I will stick to the present.

Thanks go to Jim Jacobson, Tom Scarritt and the Hansons, both Victor II and III, who took a risk on me and have my undying gratitude.

Many thanks to Tom Bailey for all his help and pestering to get this book done.

A wink and a nod and a tip of some single malt to the late Ron Casey, the greatest editorial page editor I have ever known. To Bob Blalock who could very well be the next. To Joey Kennedy, Eddie Lard and Michael Sznajderman, *The Birmingham News* editorial page staff, who make coming to work a joy and a challenge and a wonder every single day.

For Ed Stein, editorial cartoonist for the *Rocky Mountain News*, who is a friend indeed. Michael Ramirez, editorial cartoonist of the *Los Angeles Times*, who demands that I do better than I think I can.

A big hug to Copley News Services' Bob Witty, Glenda Winders and Pat Gonzalez for helping me to share my work with the world.

My father, George F. Stantis, who is my soundingboard and whose sound advice I sometimes even heed.

Spencer and Trevor Stantis, who put up with me and whom I love more than they will ever know. Until they have children themselves, at least.

If thanks were given to a single person for any success this career has afforded me it goes to my wife, Janien. She has followed my cockeyed dream across this great country for nearly two decades. She has held me in dark times when my insecurities raged and knows how to handle my raging ego. She is the best friend this cartoonist could ever want, not to mention a total hottie.

Thank you, Janien, for it all.

About the Author

Scott Stantis has been the editorial cartoonist for *The Birmingham News* since 1996. His cartoons have appeared in such varied publications as *The New York Times*, *Chicago Tribune*, *Los Angeles Times*, *Newsweek*, *National Review* and, yes, *Guns & Ammo*. He is a regular contributor to *USA Today* and *Reason* Magazine. His cartoons are syndicated to over 500 newspapers through Copley News Service. Scott is also the creator of the comic strip *The Buckets* which enjoys a client list of 100 newspapers around the world. He has been married for nearly two decades to Janien Fadich. They have two boys, Spencer and Trevor as well as a couple of dogs, Nikki and Dogzilla. Scott sits on the Board of Directors of the Epilepsy Foundation of Central and Northern Alabama. He will serve as President of the Association of American Editorial Cartoonists for the year 2002. When Scott isn't cartooning he enjoys reading, painting, writing, taking long walks with his wife and cursing his lawn.

Photo by Bernard Troncale

Send a Stantis to some friends!

Just complete the order forms below. You can cut the form out of the book, if you wish. It's just my goofy picture on the back. Or, if you can't give up my handsome pose, jot down the information on a plain piece of paper and mail it to the address listed in the form.

Please send_____copies of *Taking a Stantis* to the following address:

Name:_____

Address:_____

City, State, Zip:_____

Enclosed is my check or money order in the amount of _____(multiply the number of books you are purchasing by $16.00, which covers the book, sales tax and shipping).
To place your order, mail this coupon to:
The Birmingham News
Division of Special Projects
P.O. Box 2553
Birmingham, AL 35202
If you have questions, call 205.325.3188.
Allow 10 days for delivery.

If you wish for books to be sent to different addresses, list each address and the number of books sent to each in the space below:
Number of books:_____

Name:_____

Address:_____

City, State, Zip:_____

Number of books: _____

Name:_____

Address:_____

City, State, Zip:_____